Lucy and The Liberty Quilt

🎁 A GIFTED GIRLS SERIES™   Book 1

Lucy
AND THE
Liberty Quilt

By
Victoria London

Cover Illustration
By
Angela Liang

Published by Sparklesoup Studios
For information, please contact:
Sparklesoup Studios
P.O. Box 2285.
Frisco, TX 75034

ISBN: 0-9714776-0-4

Printed in the United States of America

This book is dedicated to Lucy, who made every sacrifice a mother could make to see her children grow up to their full potential; to Paul, who keeps me grounded in faith; to James, whose commitment on helping others and entrepreneurial spirit inspires me to reach for the skies; to Angela, whose artistic talents inspires me with my own creativity; to Tam, who has always believed in my abilities; to Oprah, who is one of the most gifted women in America; and to my wonderful husband Finlay, who makes working hard each day worth it!

Supple

Table of Contents

Foreword

God has given everyone gifts and talents.
It is the one and only Holy Spirit who
distributes these gifts.
He alone decides which gift each person should have.
— 1 Corinthians 12:11

Lucy's Prayer

Dear God,

From Huntington Beach, California (September 9, 2001) - of course you knew that already!
Here's a prayer request from Lucy, one of your favorite girls:

1. Make friends in California - my new home (although no one can replace my best friends Josie and Rachel back in New York).

2. Make better grades this year (that may need some work, but I'm willing to try).

3. Grow taller (as it is, I'm the smallest 12-year-old girl I know. God, can you somehow stretch me taller? I hope I'm not doomed to be this short forever)!

4. And finally, help make my life significant. (something spectacular, you know, God, so that I'll have some idea of what my destiny is to be).

Chapter One

Introducing Lucy!

"**Hi** everyone, I'm Lucy Lee," I said brightly to a girl with long straight dark brown hair and bright dark eyes staring back at me from my grandmother's full-length pine antique mirror. The pink flush on her cheeks was a more subdued pink than the fuchsia sweater and matching fuchsia and camel plaid miniskirt. A cable-knit pattern pale vanilla stocking covered her knees down to leather camel ankle boots. "No, too cheerful." I said aloud to myself in the mirror. "Hi folks, I'm Lucy Lee, and I'm happy as pie to be here!" I shook my head - much too country-western. After all I'm in California now, and I just moved from New York City two days ago!

I pinched myself in the mirror. I still could not believe we moved. In fact, I still could not believe some of the things that would happen next in a matter of two days. Sometimes your ordinary life can take a turn, and you find that suddenly, you are in the middle of an extraordinary adventure. That is just what happened the day I left my childhood behind, and started following my dreams - literally. It's hard to explain, so just hang tight and read on. I was just a normal girl living in California at the turn of the Millennium with dreams like all other girls - to be a princess, to be popular, to meet a cute boy, to be a movie star, to win the Nobel Peace Prize…(okay, what *I* dreamed about at age 12) when I found out that I was one of the gifted, as in the Gifted Girls.

I opened the door to my room, and looked down the

vast hallway. I was still not used to the spaciousness of our new house. Being a four-bedroom white wooden house with a rose garden, it was everything my mother, my grandmother, my little brother Peter, and I dreamed of in a home. It was so different from the little apartment we shared in Greenwich Village when my mother was an Assistant Art Professor at New York University.

"Hey, get out of my way!" said a 4-foot-tall batman-clad figure charging towards me. Too late. With my new boots, and Peter's oversized mask; both of us went flying feet first up into the sky, and landed in a tangle of blue, pink, black and camel.

"What happened," a feminine voice asked. Mom was already by Peter's side, picking him up. She was dressed in a nice burgundy wool skirt suit that enhanced her slim petite figure. Her black shoulder-length hair was curled up into a cute flip. It was Mom's first day at school, too, teaching at the University of California at Irvine as a full-fledge Professor of Art.

Peter, being only 7 years old, and overly guilt-ridden, said, "Lucy got in my way."

I stared back at Peter, and responded, "yeah, only when Peter came charging into me out of nowhere." Then I paused. "Mom, you look good!"

"Thanks," Mom said. "Now getting back to this," Mom motioned at us. "No running around in the house. I don't want to mend any broken necks and elbows this afternoon. Now you two are going to be late for school if you continue standing there. Lucy, go get some break-fast downstairs. Peter, why are you still in your pajamas?"

"I couldn't find anything to wear," Peter lied.

"Then I'll find something for you to wear," Mom said, prodding Peter towards his room.

I went down the stairs, pass the family room, and into the kitchen where Grandma had prepared a ham and cheese omelet and orange juice for me. I looked around. Grandma was nowhere to be seen. She was probably outside taking her typical slow morning stroll. I must have been hungry because I gulped down the breakfast within seconds, and headed towards the door. "Mom, I'm going now."

"Have a wonderful first day in school," Mom shouted from upstairs. In the background I heard Peter struggling with his new clothes for school. "Don't do anything I would do," he shouted.

"Uggh," I said under my breath. For a kid, he was sure obnoxious.

I headed out the door, and started walking towards the bus stop. A girl about my age with straight shoulder-length strawberry blond hair was already waiting at the corner. A tall boy with straight blond hair about 14 was waiting close to her.

I walked up next to them and smiled. "Hi," I said. "This must be the bus stop, right?"

The girl looked me up and down, and said without a smile on her face, "that's what that sign says, unless you can't read."

"Jenny," the boy said, "that's not very nice." He came over to my side, and said, "You have to excuse Jenny. Jenny's unhappy about having to take the bus to school today. Normally one of our parents take us, but they're both out-of-town for Dad's company meeting."

"Do you live around here?" I asked, immediately realizing what a dumb question it was. I thought to myself - *duh, they wouldn't be here if they didn't.*

"Actually, we live a few blocks away," the boy said.

"It took a looong time for us to get here," Jenny said

sourly. "And the bus still isn't here!"

"Well, I live just over there," I motioned to our white house. At that moment, the school bus pulled up. "Oh, the bus is here," I announced. In a way, I was glad to get away from the unpleasant Jenny, but a little disappointed to leave the friendly boy.

I entered the bus, which had about ten other children onboard, and sat in the back. The boy and Jenny boarded the bus and sat in front. The rest of the trip to school was uneventful, so I studied the back of the head of the boy who seemed so friendly. Well-formed, round head- I thought, remembering his nice dark blue eyes. Suddenly, the head I was studying turned around and looked straight at me. Embarrassed, I looked away and stared intently out the window at passing houses and streets.

When we finally got to school, I had to rush to my classroom where the teacher made me introduce myself. This was the moment I dreaded all morning.

I stood up in the middle of the room. All eyes were on me. "Hi, my name is Lucy Lee, and my family just moved here from New York," I said, hoping the ground would open up and swallow me whole. I wasn't much for speeches, and I wasn't much for making friends instantly. If it weren't for Josie and Rachel, I'd be friendless, and they were both back in New York!

I heard some giggles all around. Mrs. Jennings, our pleasant smiling history teacher, a dead ringer for Helen Hunt, announced, "Welcome Lucy. Class, let's all extend a warm welcome to our newest classmate, Lucy Lee!" At that, the class burst into a disjointed, "Welcome Lucy!"

I had to smile back. At least the teacher seemed nice. The girl sitting next to me on my left whispered over. "What made you move from New York to California?" I looked over at her briefly. She had medium brown hair and green eyes. "My mother got a job to teach Art at UC Irvine."

"Oh," the friendly girl said. "I know how it feels to be new. My family moved out here from Oklahoma about 2 years ago." Then she smiled. "I'm Renee."

"And you know who I am now," I joked.

"Yup," Renee agreed. "Nice outfit. Is that what everyone's wearing in New York now?"

I beamed. The girl had taste. "Yes. My friends Josie and Rachel will be wearing the same thing."

"I sure hope not," a familiar voice said a few chairs to my right. I looked over, and saw Jenny sticking her tongue out at me.

"What is wrong with her?" I asked Renee, not even noticing that Jenny was in the same classroom.

"Oh," Renee said, "that's Jenny. She's the richest girl in school. Her father's the president of some entertainment company. Don't mind her."

"I won't," I said, glad that at least I had found a friend in Renee. At lunch, Renee introduced me to a girl named Elsie with chin-length straight red hair and black-rimmed glasses. "This is Elsie," Renee said. "We're both working on the 6th Grade Events Committee."

"Any interest in helping us plan the Fall Festival?" Elsie asked. "This year the 6th grade is in charge of it for the whole school. Normally, the 7th grade would plan it, but we lucked out. Mrs. Jennings is our sponsor, and she convinced the Principal to let the 6th graders plan the Fall Festival this year."

"Sounds like fun," I said. "Sure, why not?"

"Good," Elsie smiled. "Looks like you have an eye for style," she motioned at my outfit. "We could use that for getting a theme together."

"Come by my house tomorrow at 3:30pm," Renee

said. "We're holding a planning meeting." She scribbled her address and phone number on the corner of some notebook paper, tore the corner, and gave it to me.

"Sure." I said, handing her my phone number, written on a piece of pink paper.

For the rest of the school day, I found myself in the same class as Jenny, whom I tried to ignore. She seemed everywhere — in the hallway, in the gym, then again at the bus stop, where her brother joined her. I kept my distance from them, hoping that would keep Jenny from looking over at me and sneering.

"Oh, hi again," the friendly boy from this morning said, approaching me. "How was your first day at school?"

"Oh," I exclaimed, surprised he knew it was my first day. "It was great! What can I say? First day at a new school is pretty nerve-wracking."

"Yeah," he said. "It must be pretty nerve-wracking, but you seem to be getting along pretty well. I heard through the grapevine that you were new in town." Then he smiled, his brown-speckled blue eyes shining. "I'm Joshua. Everyone calls me Josh."

"Well, I'm Lucy Lee," I said, noticing how his sandy blond hair flew over his tanned face.

"Lucy…I like that name," Josh said.

"Thanks," I said. "It suits me, I guess." Suddenly, I felt self-conscious talking to Josh.

"Josh," Jenny ran over, "I'm going home with Samantha and her mom. Want to come?"

Josh looked over at Jenny. "You mean you wouldn't want another trip with me on the grand bus tour?" he joked.

"You've got to be kidding," Jenny said laughing.

"I'd pass," Josh said, winking at me. "I'd rather be in a bus full of screaming children than in a Mercedes driven by that madwoman and her gossipy kid!"

"You're so dramatic," Jenny said. "I take it you don't want to come along."

"You're right, my darling sister," Josh said sarcastically.

"But Mrs. Kent will be able to drop us right in front of our house. If you take the bus, you have to walk all that way again."

Josh shook his head. "I hate to admit it, but you're making some sense. I do have to work on my artwork tonight though." He turned towards me, "I hope you don't take me leaving as being rude."

"Of course not," I said, unable to believe what a contrast he is against his rude sister.

"Good," he said smiling. "I hope to see you again, Lucy." Then he turned and joined his sister already making her way towards a red convertible Mercedes.

I hoped my mouth didn't gape as wide as I thought my eyes did, watching this nice and charmingly handsome boy walk away. What a transformation Jenny had when it came to her brother. Maybe I was just imagining all her unpleasantness earlier. Hopefully so, because her brother sure was interesting to know, and it wouldn't be that bad having a friend who lives a few blocks over.

When the bus pulled up, I was ready to go home. The afternoon was warmer than I thought, and my sweater was much too heavy. Unfortunately, I couldn't take it off. I didn't wear anything underneath except the new bra Mom bought me last week. I tugged a little on the straps underneath the sweater, trying to adjust it to fit. Bras were sure uncomfortable. I wonder how Mom and all other women wore them everyday.

I didn't have much time to imagine this when I was practically pushed into the bus by the younger kids waiting for it. I took a seat near the front this time, and pulled out a pink piece of paper. Wait until Josie hears about my first day at school, I thought, scribbling a note on the paper:

"Hi Josie. I miss you and Rachel already! How's school without me? My classes seem okay, and I have a pretty nice teacher in one of them. The kids here are nice, except for this one girl who seems to hate me. I have no idea why. But guess what??? I met this cute boy who's really nice. I know, suddenly I have some kind of interest in boys, must be my hormones...more on that later."

Chapter Two

Mrs. Potts

"Mulberry Lane," the bus driver announced. My stop. I quickly put my pen and notepad away into my backpack. The bus came to a halt, and I got off. The stop looked the same as it did this morning, but something was different. I started walking towards the direction of home, noting how the trees were a little larger than they were this morning. What a quiet street, I thought, watching a dove fly out of a tree. Then I spotted our little white house in the corner.

I walked up our steps, noticing how Grandma had already placed some flower pots on the porch, and a bird feeder. Grandma was the most energetic and independent 70-year-old I know. Thank goodness for Grandma, my mother's mother, who moved in with us after Peter was born, and Father never came home from his trip to Africa on one of his excavation trips. Father was a young archaeologist from England when Mom met him at the Met in New York. I was about 5 when he left, but I still had pictures of him, my mother, and myself on top of the World Trade Center, in front of a Christmas tree, and standing on the steps of St. Thomas Cathedral. He had wavy brown-hair and smiling green eyes. Grandma, practically raised Peter and me while Mom finished her studies in Art.

I got to the door and used my key to open the door. The key went in, but the door wouldn't open. I tried it again. The door still wouldn't open. Finally, I rang the doorbell. I heard footsteps approaching the door.

The door opened, and a short, round old woman with white hair in a bun and gentle blue eyes stood facing me with a big smile on her face. She was dressed oddly in a chiffon reddish-orange gown with gold and silver embroidery. "Oh, what a wonderful sight," she exclaimed. "He did say that 'a sudden light will appear at my door', He did," she said to herself. Then she chuckled. "He always comes through, doesn't he?"

I stood dumbfounded on the porch. The woman who opened the door was not my grandmother, and she seemed crazy in some sort of magical way! Despite all that, she seemed oddly familiar, as if I've seen her somewhere before.

"Oh, I must have forgotten." The old woman said. "With all these years, you would think I have picked up some manners. Well, allow me to introduce myself," she said with a smile. "I'm Mrs. Potts. Beatrice Potts, really, " she said with a smile, her voice had a lilt which reminded me of Julie Andrews from Mary Poppins.

"Nice to meet you, Mrs. Potts. I'm Lucy." I said. Then I shook my head. "I don't understand," I said. "I mean, where's Grandma, Mom or Peter? Aren't they home?"

"There's no one here besides me and Mr. Smithy."

"Mr. Smithy?" I asked.

"Oh yes," Mrs. Potts said. At that moment, a little black Scottish Terrier appeared at Mrs. Potts' feet. "And here's Mr. Smithy now," she said, "coming to welcome you in."

The little black dog leaped excitedly around my feet. I bent down to scratch behind his ears. He stopped leaping and stood still while he enjoyed the attention, wagging his little tail excitedly. I laughed. "He *is* cute," I said.

"And he would be very disappointed if you didn't

come in and have tea and lemon poppy seed cake with us," Mrs. Potts said lightly.

By now I had realized this was the wrong house. "I take it this isn't 351 Beachview Drive," I said.

"Oh no," Mrs. Potts said. "This is Beachview Lane," she said with a wink. "These homes around this section look very similar."

A whistling noise came from inside Mrs. Potts' house. Mr. Smithy started barking. "Looks like the tea is ready," Mrs. Potts said. "Won't you join us?"

The sweet-faced smiling Mrs. Potts and cute Mr. Smithy seemed harmless enough. I smiled. "It'll be a pleasure to have tea with such fine company," I said.

"Oh, that's wonderful!" Mrs. Potts exclaimed. She opened the door wider. "Come on in."

I followed the energetic Mrs. Potts into the house, which looked so similar to ours. But as I entered, I noticed that only the outside looked similar. Where our house still had unopened boxes all over the place, the interior of Mrs. Potts' house was painted light blue and white.

The house was furnished with colorful pottery and antique furniture. I walked over to a painting hanging over the fireplace mantel. It was an oil painting done on canvas. It was an amazing painting that showed the scattered light shining through dark clouds. A beautiful girl with flowing dark hair in a white gown stood strong and bright against the darkening sky and ragged cliffs in the painting. In one hand, she held a shield with the words, "Truth, Justice, and Charity" inscribed. In her other hand, she held another object that was blurry.

"Oh, you've found one of my favorite paintings…"Mrs. Potts came right up behind me. "It's called, *Destiny's Calling.*"

Finding my voice, I asked, "who painted this picture?"

"Why, it's Emily Cobbs," Mrs. Potts said, pointing to a signature on the bottom right corner of the painting. "She was only 12 years old when she painted *Destiny's Calling*, just an English schoolgirl living in Cambridge, England just around the turn-of-the century. She was a prodigy, they said, never touched a paint brush before she painted *Destiny's Calling*."

"Emily Cobbs?" I asked. "She was just 12 years old? But that painting looks like something in a museum, painted by someone famous, not a girl of my age. I mean, I just turned 12 years old, and I don't know anyone my age who's that talented. That's amazing!"

"Yes," Mrs. Potts said. "In fact, she just turned 12 years old when she found her sudden gift for painting. " Mrs. Potts turned towards me with a smile, "Her gift was definitely a gift from God."

I suddenly felt very shy, but I had to know more. "Mrs. Potts, how did you get the painting?"

"My mother was Emily Cobbs' good friend. Emily gave my mother this painting as a gift." Mrs. Potts gestured for me to follow her upstairs. We walked over to a room with quilts and dolls. In the middle of the room was an enormous old chest. Mrs. Potts opened the chest, and pulled out a small red velvet box. "I found it!" Mrs. Potts said. "A gift! For you!"

"My gift!" I repeated, completely surprised.

"Why of course," Mrs. Potts exclaimed. "You must have a gift for your 12th year birthday! You did say you just had a birthday, didn't you? And here it is…" She pulled out a red velvet box with a gold satin ribbon. "I had this for a while," she said, "but I could never get this ribbon off. As a messenger, I could never get this ribbon off myself. The ribbon will only open for the one it is intended. " Mrs. Potts tugged at the ribbon. She then tried cutting it, but the ribbon was as hard to cut through as steel. "See?" She then handed me the mysterious red velvet box with the unbreakable ribbon.

I touched the box gingerly, not knowing what to expect. Then I touched the edge of the golden ribbon. Something moved, and I dropped the box.

"I thought something moved," I explained, bending down to pick up the box from the ground.

"It did," Mrs. Potts said, pointing to the box. I looked at the box, and the ribbon was no longer there. Mrs. Potts started giggling like a 12 year-old. "Just what I thought! You're one of the Gifted Girls!" she exclaimed. "It's always something different. Oh, I do love my work." She laughed. "You have a card, too," she said, handing me an envelope.

I opened the heavy ivory vellum envelope and pulled out a thin golden card, which I read aloud.

"Gifts from the heart are rare but true. Gifts from above are true but few. Look inside and find one tool. First give and receive, then gifts shall come to you."

The red velvet box popped open, and revealed a small golden charm shaped like a heart with a bowtie. A golden chain ran through it as a necklace. I quickly closed the box, and handed it to Mrs. Potts. "This is weird," I said. "I can't take this."

Mrs. Potts shook her head. "I can't be mistaken. It's as clear as day. You're one of the Gifted Girls, no doubt. In a dream, I saw a child who burned brightly like a candle - 'Lucy' - your name means 'light'. It must be you. You must be the next Gifted Girl, like Emily. After all these years of recognizing Gifted Girls, I think I have more of a knack of deciphering what the clues are. This time, you practically landed on my doorstep!"

"I don't mean to be ungrateful and all," I said, "but I

just want to be a normal girl, go to school, have friends, be popular... I just started at a new school, and I'm trying hard to fit in. The last thing I want now is to stand out and be known as a freak. Am I supposed to paint something like Emily's *Destiny's Calling* now?"

Mrs. Potts shook her head and said, "Lucy, God has chosen you to be someone great. It's your destiny. You may not know what it is now."

"Do you know what it is?" I asked Mrs. Potts.

"I'm afraid I do not," she said. "That's one of the things I do not know. Every Gifted Girl has a unique gift that will be revealed in time. Because you're uniquely you, no one else is like you, Lucy, and so is your gift." Mrs. Potts smiled. "Didn't you pray for some significance in your life?"

"How do you know?" I asked, truly shocked. "I've been praying for it every night for the past seven years."

"Let's just say that I'm pretty close to Him, and He heard your prayers," Mrs. Potts wink. She handed me the golden heart necklace. "If you believe and have faith, miracles do happen." She then pulled out an old leather book from the same chest where she had pulled out the box with the golden heart necklace. "Come, Lucy, let's go into the kitchen and have some tea and poppy seed lemon cake. I have something to show you."

As I struggled between belief and disbelief, I followed Mrs. Potts down the stairs and into her sunlit kitchen that smelled of cinnamon and sweetness.

"Have a seat," Mrs. Potts said, motioning to the kitchen table with a white pitcher filled with fresh-cut sunflowers and pink daisies. Within minutes, a plate full of lemon poppy-seed cake and a steaming cup of tea was placed in front of me.

Mrs. Potts plopped herself down on the chair next to

me. "What's better on a Monday afternoon than tea and lemon poppy-seed cake?"

"This is delicious," I said, taking another bite out of my slice.

"Made it myself. Got the recipe from Daniella....oh, speaking of Daniella," Mrs. Potts opened the heavy leather book, and laid it close to me on the table. "This is Daniella." Mrs. Potts pointed to a faded black and white picture of a thin young girl with dark curls and a wide, friendly smile. She was dressed in a chef smock. On top of her head was a white chef hat. "Daniella was a Master Chef for the Royal Family of France by the age of 10 years old."

I looked closer at the picture. "She's wearing a golden heart necklace."

"Yes, like all Gifted Girls," Mrs. Potts said. "Here's a picture of Jackie from Kentucky with her horse, Spirit." I glanced down at the picture of a girl with long brown hair standing next to a horse of the same color. She was dressed in blue jeans and a red plaid shirt and boots. She, too, had a golden heart necklace around her thin neck. "Jackie had the amazing gift of understanding and healing animals." Mrs. Potts smiled. "It suited her perfectly because of her love of animals!"

After all these years of praying and believing that my prayers were being listened to, a miracle that I could hardly understand, was happening to me. Was I a complete idiot to not accept such a gift? The golden heart necklace really was very pretty, even as a necklace. If it had wonderful Gifted Girls magic, then that'll be great, too, I thought.

I looked at the photos of Daniella and Jackie and suddenly felt close to these girls with bright smiles and equally bright destinies. They accepted their destinies as

Gifted Girls, maybe I should, too!

I turned towards Mrs. Potts. "I don't know why God chose me to be a Gifted Girl, and what is my gift? I don't understand what I'm supposed to do as a Gifted Girl, too. But I don't think I can choose not to be one, too, knowing that I have this extraordinary gift that is meant to be used."

"That's it, Lucy," Mrs. Potts said. "God will trust you to know when to use it and when not to. You may make mistakes. After all, you're not perfect, we all aren't (even if you're a Gifted Girl). But you'll learn." Mrs. Potts stopped. "I bet He has a wonderfully fabulous gift in store for you! I can't wait for you to discover it!"

I smiled. "Well, Mrs. Potts, if it's destiny, and I have this gift that God wants me to use, I guess I will become a Gifted Girl."

"I'm glad you accepted." Mrs. Potts took the necklace out of the box. "Happy Birthday!" She exclaimed, "and a true new birth day it is!" She then fastened the necklace around my neck. She lifted her teacup and said, "Here's to a wonderful life."

I lifted my teacup in return, "to a wonderful life." A grandfather clock in the living room started chiming 4 o'clock. "But first I have to find my way home before everyone starts wondering where I am."

"Of course," Mrs. Potts said. Mr. Smithy ran over to see if there were any leftover cake crumbs on the ground. "It's time for you to go home."

I finished my cake and the tea. "Sorry, Mr. Smithy, but that cake was too delicious to share," I said. Then I grabbed my bag, put the necklace inside and headed towards the door. Mrs. Potts and Mr. Smithy came with me.

"I live close by," Mrs. Potts said. "You're welcome to come by and share a cup of tea and cake with me anytime," she said.

"Thanks," I said. "For the necklace and cake, you know."

"I know," Mrs. Potts said. "Now, to get home, just head on back to the corner, turn left, go down two streets, and you should find your house!"

"Thanks again," I said making my way towards the corner. "I'll come and visit again, I'm sure," I waved. Then I quickened my pace. I should've been home by 3:30. Mom and Grandma would be worried. I still had to help unpack everything and do my homework.

I quickly found my way home, and found Grandma in the kitchen preparing some wonderful Chinese egg rolls. Grandma's egg rolls were my favorite dish. When Grandma and Grandpa ran a Chinese restaurant in Chinatown in New York, Grandma's egg rolls were one of the most popular dishes in town. When Grandpa passed away, Grandma sold the restaurant, and retired. Now Mom, Peter, and I have the good fortune of having a famous chef cook for us everyday!

"Hi Lu-cee," Grandma called from the kitchen. "School went okay?"

I plopped down at our modern art deco kitchen table, which looked so different than Mrs. Potts' antique walnut table. Already on the table was a dish of egg rolls and sauce. "For you," Grandma said with a smile. She loved feeding me.

"Oh school went pretty well," I said. "You know, first day. I'm still trying to get used to being in California."

Grandma nodded. "California is so different from New York. You miss your friends? Jo-see? Rachel?"

"I sure do, Grandma," I said. I missed my best friends, but at the same time, I also understood what a great opportunity it was for Mom to get her job. "But I'm making some friends here, now," I said brightly, hoping to sound positive. "In fact, I think I have some already!" Then I described how friendly Renee was, how smart Elsie was, and how friendly Josh was. I didn't want to describe Mrs. Potts yet. I think that's one secret I wanted to keep for myself.

"See," Grandma said. "Already making friends. First day, too." She laughed. "I walked this morning. Walked pretty far, but I found a church with people having breakfast. Morning service, I think. Made some friends myself," Grandma winked. "They invited me to come back again."

At that moment, the door opened, and Mom blew in with Peter in tow. "Sorry I'm late," Mom said. "This guy here," Mom said, pointing to Peter, "got into a fight with some boys. On the first day of school, too!"

"It wasn't my fault," Peter wailed. "They started making fun of me at recess so I started kicking one of them, then they ganged up on me." Grandma took one look at Peter's black eye, and then came back with some ointment. "Ouch," Peter said. "They were all bigger than me, too. But I fought better than any of them. If I look bad, you should see what happened to them!" he said proudly.

"Okay, Peter," Mom said. "That's enough about the fight. I'm meeting with one of the boys' parents tomorrow. The principal will be there and hopefully, that'll nip things in the bud."

Grandma came over to the table with more dishes heaping with egg rolls. "Now this is for you," she said to my mother, "And you, Peter."

"Yummy," Peter said, rushing to the table. "Nothing beats Grandma's cooking."

Mom said, "That's true," dropping her briefcase and

bag down on the sofa and heading towards upstairs. "I need to get out of this suit and into something more comfortable," she said.

I finished my dish, and got up. "I have to do homework and unpack," I told Grandma and Peter.

Grandma said, "No need to unpack. Go do homework, Lu-cee. I already unpacked for you." I rushed up the stairs to my room, and found the boxes from this morning gone, clothes neatly folded in my dresser, and my collection of dolls and stuffed animals neatly piled up on my window seat. Grandma was amazing. "Thanks, Grandma," I shouted. "You're the best!" Then I threw my backpack on top of my yellow-coverlet bed and plopped down next to it. I reached in to retrieve my notebook and my U.S. history textbook. Mrs. Jennings asked us to write a one-page paper on what we thought was one of the most significant times in American history. I opened my history book, and thumbed through the contents. Everything seemed pretty significant, I thought, going through the contents.

I reached into my bag for a highlighter pen, and found my red velvet box with the golden heart necklace. How could I have forgotten about it? I put on the necklace, wondering what I should write for the paper. Then I flipped through the pages, stopping to read some of the chapters. Slowly, but surely, my eyes started feeling heavy, and soon they were closed in deep sleep.

Chapter Three

Day of Infamy

I must have fallen asleep after I wrote my paper because when I woke up, my paper was written and complete. I had written about the American Revolution and how significant the American Flag was in symbolizing America's fight for freedom. I stuffed the paper into my backpack, and got ready for school. I chose a red long-sleeve t-shirt with my denim overalls, red socks, and white sneakers. As I made my way down the stairs, Grandma and Mom were already in the family room, watching the morning news.

"Good morning!" I said, glad that my homework assignment was complete.

Mom and Grandma didn't answer. Instead, their eyes were glued to the television. Then Mom saw me, and walked over. Her face looked worried. "Lucy, you're not going to school today," she said gently. "Schools and universities are going to be closed today."

"Why?" I asked, "September 11 isn't a holiday, is it?"

"No," Mom said, "but it'll go down in American history someday as a day of infamy." Mom took a breath. "America was attacked this morning."

"What?" I asked, not understanding what Mom was telling me. I walked over to the television to see what was going on.

That was when I saw replay footage of an airplane crashing into New York's World Trade Center. And then a second plane crashing into the second tower.

For a horrifying second, I couldn't breathe. This could not be happening, I thought.

Then a news anchorman said in a shaky, but calm voice that it appears that the crash was deliberate, and that it could be the act of terrorists. Then he repeated the news from a few minutes ago. "This morning," the distinguished anchorman said, "two commercial airplanes have crashed into the Twin Towers of the World Trade Center. One commercial airplane has just crashed into the Pentagon. And the first tower has collapsed." I stood transfixed, unable to move, as I watched the First Tower collapse and the screen filled with a heavy dark gray smoke. The world spun around me, and I had tears in my eyes. My old home, New York, was being attacked by terrorists.

Mom was already on the phone, calling people we knew in New York. Grandma sat silently on the sofa with her head bent down, eyes closed.

Minutes later, the news anchorman announced that another plane had crashed into the countryside of Pennsylvania.

Mom came back into the family room. Relief written all over her face. "Cousin Arnie and his family's fine," she announced about our second cousin who worked in the Wall Street area of New York near the World Trade Center.

Moments later, everyone gasped as the news showed the second tower of the World Trade Center come crashing down. "All those people," Grandma said. "So senseless."

"Josie and Rachel," I said. "I have to find out if they're alright." I grabbed the phone, and dialed Josie's number. Her father was a firefighter for the New York City Fire Department.

My fingers began dialing her familiar number. She seemed so far away, but suddenly so close. The phone on the other end began ringing. Then a woman's voice answered, "Hello? Is this Ed?"

"No," I said, "I'm Lucy, Mrs. Beretti, is Josie there?"

"Oh," Mrs. Beretti, Josie's mother said, "No, she's still in school. I'm going to get her. She should be fine, though. School's a bit of a ways away from the World Trade Center. It's her father I'm worried about. He's headed over to help rescue and aid those in the Center, God bless them."

"I'll say a prayer for his and Josie's safety," I told Mrs. Beretti.

"Thanks," she said. "Prayers are what we need right now. God help us."

"I know. God help us," I prayed. "I'll clear the line so you can hear from Mr. Beretti."

"That'll be good," Mrs. Beretti said. "I'll tell Josie you called."

"Okay. Take care. And tell her I miss her!" I hung up the phone. Then I dialed Rachel's number. The line rang and rang. Finally, the answering machine picked up. "Hi, Rachel, this is Lucy. Just calling to see if you're alright. I miss you, girl!" Rachel was probably in school with Josie, and Rachel's parents, both doctors in New York City, probably busy helping out at hospitals near the disaster site.

I returned to the family room where the news was showing an evacuation of the areas surrounding the collapsed buildings. Peter was on Mom's lap. He was dressed in a blue plaid shirt His face was streaming with tears. "What if they attack us?" Peter wailed. He was clearly scared.

"We have to trust that our government is doing the

best they can to protect us," Mom said gently.

"Oh wait," I said, "the news said that all commercial flights were canceled or routed to Canada." I went over to Peter, and patted him on the shoulder. "See? Our government knows what to do." For some reason, giving Peter some minor reassurance helped calm my fears.

Grandma got up. "Everyone. Go have breakfast. We have work to do. Everyone needs food to be strong."

"What?" I asked.

Grandma went to the kitchen and heated up all the dishes that had gone cold earlier. "Lu-cee and Peter eat up. We all go to church. They have a prayer meeting. My new friend Lucia called me and said people are getting to church for prayer."

Mom perked up, "that's a good idea."

I grabbed Peter and propelled him towards our kitchen table. Grandma had already placed a bowl of oatmeal with cinnamon and sugar at our spot at the table with a glass of milk. I tasted the creamy oatmeal, and gulped it down quickly with the glass of milk. I didn't realize how hungry I was. Peter ate slower and remained quiet.

When we were done, Mom and Grandma waited for us at the door, heading out to the driveway and garage. Mom opened the garage, and we piled into Mom's black sport utility vehicle.

"Mom," Mom said to Grandma, "since you know where the church is, you lead the way."

"Okay," Grandma said. "Go to corner of street, turn right at stop, then go down following street."

As Mom followed Grandma's direction, I noticed how quiet Peter was. "Hey," I elbowed him slightly. "Don't be scared."

Peter turned towards me. "We're going to go fight back, aren't we?" he asked.

"Maybe, most likely," I said. "After all. We were attacked. That's an act of war. America needs to stop it from ever happening again. It's unpleasant, but sometimes we have to do unpleasant things to prevent further unpleasant things," I said, surprised how calm and mature I sound.

"I wished Dad was here," Peter said wistfully. "I don't want to be the only man to protect everyone in the family."

"I do, too," I said. "Especially, if you have to protect us. That would really be scary," I joked.

"Hey," Peter said. "That's not fair. Just because I'm small…"

"…and scrawny, and most of all, ticklish," I said, reaching over to tickle Peter on his stomach, under his arms, everywhere. He was a ball of ticklish nerves. Peter couldn't stop laughing, and had tears coming out of his eyes.

"Well, guys," Mom said, "here we are!"

I stopped tickling Peter, and looked out the window. The building we were pulling up to was large. It was a modern building and reminded me of a school.

"This is campus," Grandma said. "Church has so many things here - mission trips, youth groups, young adults, children, counseling…that big building there is the main church."

"Sanctuary," Mom said. "Wow, what a nice church."

There were cars already on the lot. Some more cars were pulling in like we were. We found a place to park near the entrance, and walked inside. A woman with short blond hair, a sweater, and slacks greeted Grandma at the entrance to the sanctuary.

"This is Lucia," Grandma said.

"Glad you could come out here," she said.

Grandma proudly introduced my Mom, Peter, and I to

Lucia. "My daughter, grandson, and granddaughter," she said.

"Well, good to meet all of you," Lucia said. "This is last minute, but we opened the church up for anyone who needed comfort and prayers." Lucia took one look at Peter. "It's alright to be scared. It's a scary time, and that's why we need to start praying."

Chapter Four

Prayers for New York

I looked around the lobby of the sanctuary. The lobby was airy with stained glass and polished wood everywhere. It felt comfortable and peaceful, as if I needed to be here.

As we made our way into the sanctuary, I noticed a young man, standing by a wall, with his head down. I stopped walking. I could recognize that head anywhere. It was Josh!

I told Mom, Grandma, Lucia, and Peter that I'll join them later. Then I approached Josh.

"Josh?" I asked.

The young man lifted his head. "Lucy?" He blinked his eyes. His eyes were red as if he had been crying. "What are you doing here?"

"I felt like I should be here, rather than at home. I'm here with my mother, grandmother, and brother. Where's Jenny?"

Josh wiped his eyes. "She's with a counselor right now. She took this all pretty hard." Josh stopped. "You know, we think our parents may have been on one of those flights. We're not sure, but so far we haven't been able to get in touch with anyone who would know."

"I'm so sorry to hear that," I said sincerely. The event this morning had changed so many lives. I reached up and touched his shoulder. "If you need to talk to anyone, I'm here," I said.

"Thanks," Josh said. "I'm glad you are, too." He looked at me intently, and my heart skipped a beat. "I'm glad you moved out here. You know, you'd be a good influence on Jenny."

"Oh," I said, feeling disappointed.

Josh said, "There's a strong possibility that they weren't on any of those flights, too. I just pray they weren't."

"Me, too," I said. "My friend Josie's father's in New York right now with the rest of his Fire Unit, and my other friend Rachel's parents work at a hospital near the disaster site. I'm worried about them, too."

Josh reached out and gave me a hug. I hugged him back. It felt comfortable in his arms. "Hey," he said. "Let's go into the sanctuary and join the others. I think we all need some comfort."

"I agree," I said quickly, not wanting him to see how disappointed I was in ending this too short of an interlude with Josh, who I now was definitely convinced was the cutest and coolest boy I knew. Josh and I headed towards an empty pew and sat down.

"That's Pastor Jennings," Josh said, pointing at the white-haired man in a sweater at the front of the sanctuary. "He's the Senior Pastor of this church. Also the father-in-law of Mrs. Jennings, your history teacher."

"I know this morning's event has shaken many of our lives," Pastor Jennings said. "And a lot of you are scared. Let me tell you, I'm scared, too," Pastor Jennings said. "But we can find strength and comfort in our Lord," he said. "Our doors are open for all faith to come and pray for strength and guidance. To pray for America. To pray for President Bush and our leaders. To pray for comfort and peace of mind. For all those who were in the World Trade Center, the Pentagon, the airplanes. Our firefighters, our rescue workers, our police and security forces..."

I looked over at Josh and saw his head bent in prayer. I bent my head, and closed my eyes, and whispered a prayer myself.

A beep started. "Is that you, God," I thought. "I'm supposed to be gifted, but I feel so helpless." I opened my eyes.

Josh had a cell phone in his hand. "Excuse me," he said. He then walked out into the lobby.

I resumed my prayer. "I don't know what my gift is or how to use it, but I do want to use it to help." I touched my golden heart charm. It felt warm. Suddenly, my face felt flushed. It must be getting warm in here, I thought. My forehead started sweating, and I felt weak. *Need air*, I thought. *Must have some air.* I looked up at the roof of the sanctuary, at the stained glass portrait of a cross and a dove. So peaceful, I thought, and then everything turned black.

Chapter Five

Lucy's Discovery

I read somewhere before that dreams have a way of revealing answers. At the moment I blacked out, I dreamt one of those dreams about the girl in Emily's painting, 'Destiny's Calling'. It went like this...

A young girl with flowing black hair and bright dark eyes stood on the shores of a rocky beach. This day the sky has turned dark gray, and the wind was gushing rain. The girl is dressed in a flowing white sheer gown, tied at the waist by a blue sash. With her porcelain skin and willowy figure, she looked delicate and regal like a Princess from an old fairy tale. But something in her eyes and her mouth showed determination and strength. She was trained to be a warrior. In one hand, she held a sharp needle as large as a sword. In her other hand, she held a shield.

She gestured towards me, mouthing words I could barely hear. "Lu," I heard her say. I moved closer. "Lucy" she says in a calm, gentle voice. She ran up the shore to a natural ditch on the beach. She then gestured for me to follow. I took a step. The rocks on the ground were too sharp for my slippers. She gestured for me to hurry. I clenched my teeth, and moved forward, the rocks biting into my feet. Finally, after what seemed like a painful eternity, I was shoulder to shoulder with her. "It is time," she said. Then she pointed over to the horizon. The rain had subsided, but a large dark cloud had formed, unlike any I have ever seen.

The girl turned towards me. A sudden weariness washed over her face. She handed me the needle. "May your needle protect you and keep your enemies away." She then handed me the shield. "May the shield of truth, justice, and charity guide you and lead you through people's hearts." She then touched my face. "You must go," she said. "towards the cloud. You will know what to do."

"But what is it?" I asked, my heart thumping with the dread of the inevitable.

"No time now. I cannot explain to you. You will understand," the Princess Warrior said. "Go!" Then she pushed me forward towards the cloud, so hard that I stumbled and fell. I got up, turned around, but the Princess Warrior had left. "Wait," I shouted. "What am I supposed to do? Come back!"

"Lucy?" a male voice shook me out of my dream.

"What?" I jerked up suddenly. I opened my eyes and realized that I was still sitting in the pew.

Josh was sitting by me. "Hey," he said, "I have some good news. My parents just called. They were supposed to fly out of Boston tomorrow, not today so Jenny and I were mistaken about their flights, thank God."

"That's wonderful news," I said, giving him a hug.

"I know," Josh said. "That was so close. It made me realize how much I love my parents, you know." He got up. "I have to tell Jenny. She's going to be so relieved."

"Take care," I said.

Josh took my hand. "Lucy, thanks for being here. You don't know how much of a comfort it was for me to be able to share my fears with someone and to pray with someone at that moment."

"Well, that's what a friend is for," I said.

Josh's face lighten up. "Yes, definitely. Friends." He

handed me a small slip of paper. I looked down at it. His number! "Call me if you need anything." He got up and left.

I got up and headed towards one of the rooms at the church. I wanted to be alone. And this room seemed perfect to collect my thoughts. I looked around. Apparently I was in some sort of craft room. Colorful paper, markers, fabric, beads, ribbons, threads, and yarn popped out of bags strewn all over the room.

Although I've never sewed anything in my life, I headed towards one of the largest bags, pulled out a large black satin fabric, grabbed a pair of scissors and a needle with thread. Within minutes, I had sewn a full black evening gown with a heavily beaded bodice and a matching satin drawstring bag.

I pulled another fabric out of another bag. This time, it was a red velvet material. Within minutes, this material was transformed into a cape, fit for an emperor, with gold and silver embroidery. Next I pulled out a lavender chiffon material. With just a flick of my wrist and the needle in my finger, the chiffon became a skater's outfit. In a matter of 5 minutes, I had completed 10 outfits.

I stopped. My golden heart necklace was burning hot. I took it off, and left it on the table. This gave me a chance to survey what I had done. What *had* I done? I surveyed the work I had just created, unable to believe my eyes. It was as if my fingers had a mind of their own. Besides the black evening gown, emperor's cape, and skater's outfit, I had sewn a Colonial cotton dress, a safari jacket with shorts, a Victorian lace dress, a three-piece pantsuit, a medieval gown with cap, a cowgirl's outfit, and a clown costume.

I touched the hem of the Colonial dress, admiringly. It was made as if by an expert seamstress with over 20 years of experience. Without a second thought, I slipped the dress on. It fit perfectly! I pranced around in the costume, enjoying how feminine it made me feel. "Why, I would accept your dance, Mr. Josh," I pretended. Then I slipped the golden heart necklace on and gathered my long hair under the white cotton cap that goes with the dress. There. I looked like a colonial girl in the 1770s, when America's early founders were alive. I closed my eyes, feeling the room spin around.

When I opened my eyes again, I was sitting on an uncomfortable wood chair besides a very large wood table in a plain white room. Around the table were other girls dressed in colonial costumes like mine.

The girl next to me handed me a needle and thread. "Here you go," she said. She had curly brown hair with warm brown eyes. "Aunt Betsy would be glad you showed up to help sew. Since the war began, it is even more important to finish the flag."

I stared at the girl. "What war?"

The girl said, "Why the Revolutionary War, of course, between the American colonists and England."

Revolutionary War? "What year are we in?"

The girl with the merry face looked at me. "The year of our Lord 1776." She looked sidewise at me. "Why Lucy, you have not forgotten where we are, as well? If so, you really have not fully recovered from your illness and should be in bed. You do know we are in Aunt Betsy's upholstery house in Philadelphia, and that I am Virginia, unless you have forgotten *that*, too?"

I coughed. "Why, yes, it's all coming back to me now," I faked. "Of course I remember, Virginia."

"Good," Virginia laughed. "I wouldn't know what to do if my friend had to be bedridden for another week. My sister Rosalind and mother had been going on incessantly about Rosalind's wedding. Now that you are well, you will be a welcome relief from all that fussing and primping."

"I agree," I said. "So why are we here today?"

"Aunt Betsy has asked me to help her with sewing a flag. She needs as much help as possible since General Washington commissioned her to sew the first official flag of this country."

Boy, I was sure glad I read that chapter on the American Revolution for history class last night. "Aunt Betsy?"

"Yes, my Uncle Ross' wife. They run an upholstery business, and Aunt Betsy was fortunate enough to know General George Washington and his family. They're members of Betsy's church."

At that moment, a small woman with a strong face and dark hair in a bun walked into the room, carrying strips of fabric and stars. She was a young woman about the age of 24 years old.

Virginia glanced over at the young woman. "There's Aunt Betsy now." She started waving. The young woman dropped off the supplies she was carrying at the edge of the table, glanced over and smiled. She made her way around the table to our side and gave Virginia a hug, her face beaming.

"Another generation joins the upholstery business," Aunt Betsy said laughing. "And you've brought a friend."

Virginia excitedly joined in, "My best friend, Lucy! She's come back from the brink of death to help out with the war effort."

I blushed. "You're so dramatic!" I said. "I was ill, but now I'm here, happy to help out wherever I can, urrhh…"

"Betsy," Aunt Betsy said, "Betsy Ross, but you can call me Aunt Betsy."

"Aunt Betsy," I said, relishing how simple it was to call her Aunt Betsy. I smiled back at this young woman with a warm personality who would go down in history as a woman whose work would spur Americans to fight, spur Americans to live, even spur Americans to go to the moon!

Aunt Betsy patted my shoulder. "I'm glad to have such dedicated young workers here today." She smiled particularly at me, "even ones who are so dramatic."

"I am not," Virginia exclaimed. "I am just young and energetic."

"Now let's use some of that youthful energy with this flag we're sewing here," Aunt Betsy said. She grabbed some fabric and placed it in front of us. "We need some stars for the flag." She showed us a drawing of the finished flag. Thirteen stars in a circle, representing the thirteen colonies in America. "You get to cut the stars," Aunt Betsy said. She handed each of us a pair of scissors. "Here are the patterns." Then she left and walked over to the other girls in the room.

"Well," I said to Virginia, "let's get started." I grabbed one of the star patterns, placed it down on the fabric, and began tracing the patterns onto the fabric.

I looked over at Virginia. She did the same thing. "My mother should be proud," Virginia said. "It is the first time I touched a piece of fabric that did not end up having to be mended."

"Oh, we'll just wait and see," I joked. "Now let's see what happens when we actually cut the fabric." I took a snip. Virginia did, too. Then we took additional snips until we had a few stars on the table.

Aunt Betsy came by and pulled us aside. "Come take a break with me," she whispered. "I have a pitcher of lemonade in the parlor and a whole freshly-baked apple cinnamon pie."

"That'll be wonderful!" Virginia exclaimed. "Sweets! Mother says that it is a good thing I did not know how to bake. If I had mastered the art, I could not be able to stop myself from eating everything I made." She led me to Aunt Betsy's parlor.

Unlike the harshness of the sewing room, the parlor was a sumptuous array of silk damask pillows on silk sofas and antique ivory lace curtains. "Aunt Betsy had this room decorated like the latest European design," Virginia said. "This is where she receives her customers and guests so it should be impressive."

The parlor room looked warm and inviting, smelling of fresh apples. In the middle of the room, already helping himself to a large slice of apple pie was a tall older gentleman dressed completely in black.

Aunt Betsy came into the parlor with some papers. "I see you've already found the apple pie," she said to the tall impressive older gentleman.

"I could not refuse such hospitality," the gentleman joked back. "Especially when such luxury is so rare to find."

"Oh, George," Aunt Betsy said. "Help yourself to more then!" Then she turned to us. "Except leave a bite or two for my two girls there."

Virginia and I moved up to the tall gentleman and shook his hand.

"General Washington," Aunt Betsy said. "Here are your latest recruits for the war effort - my niece Virginia and her best friend Lucy. They are young, but willing. And, according to young Virginia there, full of youthful energy."

"So," General Washington said, "You have a heart for America's fight for freedom?"

"Yes, sir," I said, looking George Washington in the eyes.

"Good, we need to be strong during this time," he said. "Freedom from tyranny comes with a price, but to all who wish to be known as Americans, it is a price worth fighting for." He sat down in one of the pink demure sofas, his enormous size made the sofa looked even smaller. "The flag will be an important part of the war," General Washington said. "When Americans see the flag, they will be reminded of everything America stands for - justice, freedom, and separation from oppression. Winning the Revolutionary War begins in our hearts. Are you helping your Aunt Betsy with the flag?"

"Yes, sir," Virginia said. "Lucy and I have just cut a few stars."

"Stars?" General Washington asked.

"Yes," Aunt Betsy said. "While the girls help themselves to the apple pie, let's go over the design of the flag." She handed General Washington the papers she was holding.

Meanwhile, Virginia and I went over and grabbed pieces of the pie, poured two cups of lemonade, and sat in the corner of the room. We were finished in seconds. We then stood up, left Aunt Betsy with General Washington deep in discussion about business and went back to work in the sewing room.

The room was buzzing with chatter and laughter. The girls were enjoying themselves. I smiled, and went back to cutting stars. By the end of the day, Virginia and I had finished cutting several stars.

Virginia got up, and stretched. "Lucy, I'm afraid I have to take my leave. Mother is expecting me for dinner, actually I have to help make dinner, everyone is busy with the preparations for Rosalind's wedding." She grabbed my hands. "Thank you, Lucy, for helping Aunt Betsy and I today. We are truly grateful." Then she left.

I looked around the room. Everyone was getting ready to leave for the day. Stars and fabric pieces were piled high on the table, ready for sewing. I got up and walked over to a window in the room. The room had gotten stuffy. I tried opening the window, but found it was tightly shut. I needed some air again. This time, I touched my golden heart necklace, and closed my eyes.

When I opened my eyes, I was back in the craft room at church. I smiled. I was finally getting accustomed to the golden heart necklace. I quickly changed out of my Colonial dress and back into my denim overalls. I piled the 10 outfits I created into a bag, and went out looking for my family.

I found Mom, Grandma, Peter, and Lucia in the lobby. "Oh, here is Lucy," Mom said.

"Hi," I said, wondering how long I've been gone.

"We're heading home," Mom said. "President Bush just made an announcement about the attacks. He said most likely it was the act of terrorists, and the U.S. Government will take action against those behind it. In the meanwhile, America is fuming mad. We have to continue on with our lives or the bad ones will win."

"So, we're heading home," Peter said. "I'm getting hungry."

"Let's go," Mom said. We said good-bye to Lucia, and headed for Mom's car.

On the way home, the car buzzed with excited chatter. Mom was very impressed by the church's design and style. Peter liked Pastor Jennings, and Grandma liked how we went as a family to church. I listened to everyone's praise of the church, but was lost in my own thoughts. Betsy Ross and General Washington had given me an idea.

Chapter Six

The Liberty Quilt

When we reached home, I ran up the stairs to my room, tugging my bag of outfits behind me. I placed the bag in a corner of my closet, behind the large teddy bear my father had given me when I was 5 years old.

I took off the golden heart necklace, placed it in the first drawer of my dresser. Then I grabbed my pink notebook.

I walked down the stairs. Grandma was in the kitchen preparing lunch. Peter was right beside her, helping. I did a double-take. Peter helping prepare lunch? That was new.

Mom came into the kitchen with the cordless phone. "Lucy, it's for you."

"Thanks," I said, taking the phone. "Hello?"

"Lucy!" a screamed came from the phone. Rachel. "How are you doing, girlfriend?" she asked. "I returned home and found your message on the machine. School was let out early today. I mean how could anyone think about school today?"

"I'm glad you're okay," I said. "How's everyone in your family?"

"Oh, we're fine, thank God. Mom and Dad's over near the disaster site. They're going to be there all night, I think, hoping that they could help anyone who needs it."

"Heard from Josie, yet?"

"Josie was with me at school, but then she went home

with her mother." Rachel fell silent for a while. "Her father's at Ground Zero. His unit was one of the first ones to go into the Towers."

"Is he out yet?"

"Josie hasn't heard anything since this morning. We're all worried about him." Rachel stopped. "Boy, I sure wish you were here. It's not safe to go out right now. Otherwise, I'd go right on over to Josie's place."

"I know," I said. "You know Josie, how responsible and organized she is. If she gets a chance, she'll call us. I'm glad you're both fine, though. It feels so weird being out here in California when you're all back there."

"Pretty scary," Rachel said. "But, hey, together, we'll pull through, right?"

"Right," I said. "Hey, I got an idea to help show our support for our friends, for our nation, the family of the victims..." Then I proceeded to tell her of my idea. "Can you help organize this from the schools on your end? You and Josie?"

"Sounds big, but it can be done," Rachel said.

"Now I just need to get the word out to all the schools from New York to California," I said.

"Fabulous," Rachel said. "You can count on me!"

"I know," I said. "Now I have some calls to make."

"Same here," Rachel said. "Talk to you later. Bye."

"Bye, Rachel," I said. "Stay safe."

I opened up my notebook, and found Elsie's phone number. I quickly dialed the number. A man answered the phone. "Hello?"

"Is Elsie there?" I asked.

The man called Elsie's name. "Elsie, it's for you." Then I heard Elsie's voice close to the phone. "Thanks, Dad, I won't be long. I know you're waiting to hear from Uncle Jack."

"Hello?" Elsie's matter-of-fact voice asked.

"Hi, Elsie?" I said. "It's Lucy."

"Oh, Lucy," Elsie said. "The Fall Festival meeting's been canceled for today because of everything that's happening."

"I figure," I said. "When we do meet, though, I definitely have an idea for the Fall Festival."

"Great!" Elsie said. "That was fast. You're pretty creative."

"Well, wait until you hear the idea before you think it's great," I said.

"I'm all ears," Elsie said. "Better yet. Hold the thought. You live on Beachview Drive, right?"

"Right," I said.

"I'm actually a few blocks away. I'll grab Renee, and we'll be right over. The Fall Festival must go on!" Elsie laughed. "The meeting is on again, I guess," Elsie said. "See you soon."

"See you soon," I said.

Then I pulled out a piece of paper from my pocket. Josh's number. I dialed the number quickly. If we begin soon, we can have the project ready by the Fall Festival, I calculated. But if I were to use my gift of sewing, because it was obviously the gift I'm supposed to have as a Gifted Girl, the project could be completed quickly. So tempting. I shook my head. The beauty of the project was the work of others, not just myself.

The phone rang, and a girl's voice answered. "Hello?" I could recognize that voice anywhere. Jenny.

I almost hung up the phone. "Hi," I said. "Is Josh there?"

"Josh!" Jenny shouted. "Phone." Then she turned towards the phone. "Who is calling?"

"Lucy," I said, hoping Jenny doesn't hang up.

"Lucy?" Jenny said. Then there was silence. "Ah, about my brother," she said. "I want to thank you for praying with him today," she said.

I wiped my eyes. Was I dreaming or did Jenny, who seemed to hate me, just thanked me?

"Uh, thanks," I said, shakily. This was weirder than me going back to the Colonial Days and meeting Betsy Ross and George Washington this morning.

"Lucy?" a friendly male voice said.

"Josh?" I said, hoping I didn't sound overly anxious in hearing his voice over the phone. "Hey, I wanted to know how everything is."

"Oh," Josh said. Did he sound disappointed? "Thanks for asking. Mom and Dad's trying to catch the first flight home, but all the flights have been canceled for today."

"That's good to hear." I said. Then I took a breath. "Do you want to come over? I live close to the bus stop, remember where we first met?"

"Is this like a date?"

"Oh, no," I said.

"Oh," Josh said.

"I mean," I felt embarrassed. Maybe I should just hang up now. "I have an idea for the Fall Festival for School, and I thought you might be interested in helping out. I thought I heard you're into Art."

"I am," Josh said quickly. "It's actually my passion."

"Then come on over at 3 o'clock sharp," I said, "unless you have something else to do."

"No, not really," Josh said. "Sure. I'll be right over at 3."

"Bring Jenny along, too," I said. "She'll probably enjoy it."

"Okay, I'll ask her," Josh said. "See you at 3."

"Bye," I said, smiling into the phone. That was easy,

thank goodness. Then I went into the kitchen.

"Grandma...that idea about us going to church for the prayer meeting was great! So great, that I've invited a few of my new friends over later for another meeting."

Grandma smiled. "That's good. Good thing to do." Then she smiled wisely. "Grandma will make some of her famous pastry puffs for snack, then."

I smiled. "That's a great idea, Grandma. I'm sure everyone would be eating up a plateful."

Grandma said. "That's okay." She put her arms around Peter's shoulders. "I have a little helper tonight."

"Yeah," Peter said. "Grandma's teaching me how to cook and make all sort of yummy things!"

I walked over and ruffled Peter's hair. "Hey, hey," he said, "no messing with the Chef's hair. No wonder why chefs wear that tall white hat."

Then I walked over to the study where Mom was busy at the computer. Mom had converted the study into a mini-studio for Mom's art projects and an office where Mom worked on her class projects. Besides being an Art Professor, Mom operated an internet art gallery that sells her and her student's artwork.

"Mom," I said, "I'm having some friends over this afternoon. We're going to work on an art project that I think will help benefit the victims of this morning's attacks."

Mom stopped working and came over. "Why Lucy, that's a great idea! I'm so glad you have an interest in art. Do you need me to help out in any way?"

"Well, Mom," I said. "I actually do. Can you sit in on the meeting we're having this afternoon? It's at 3. Grandma and Peter's preparing some snacks for the meeting, too!"

"Of course, sweetie," Mom said. "I'll be there. Just

let me finish this paper for my class, then you can have all my attention for the rest of the day."

"Okay," I said. "They should be here in a few minutes. That'll give you some time, right," I joked.

"Uhhh," Mom said. "Then I really have to work."

"Okay...I'm leaving," I said. Then I went to the family room where the television was still broadcasting the attack from this morning. "Please God, help Josie's father, Mr. Beretti, be safe," I prayed. I stared at the screen, still unable to believe the once magnificent Twin Towers of the World Trade Center reduced to rubble. Still unbelievable was that there were thousands of people still in the building when the Towers crashed. Somewhere out there was Josie's father.

The doorbell rang. "I'll get it," I shouted. I checked my hair in the mirror in the hallway, and opened the door. Renee and Elsie stood awkwardly outside. "Renee! Elsie! Come on in," I said.

Elsie walked in first, taking in the entire house. "Nice house," she said.

Renee came in next. "Cool painting," she said pointing at one of Mom's oil canvases hanging in the family room.

"Thanks," I said. "Mom would be glad to hear that. She decorated the house, and the painting's one of her originals."

"She's an artist?" Elsie asked.

"Well, I try to be," Mom said, walking in to join us.

"Mom, this is Elsie and Renee from school." I said. Then I turned to the girls, "Elsie and Renee, this is Mom."

"Glad to meet you, Mrs. Lee," they both said in unison.

"Same here," Mom said. "Hey, let me show you around the house."

Grandma came into the room with a plate of warm pastry puffs and handed it to me. "For your friends," she said and disappeared.

The doorbell rang, and I went to answer the door. I opened the door. Josh was wearing a light blue sweater that emphasized his blue eyes and jeans. He looked just like a model for a sensitive Californian surfer - all American. "Hi Josh," I said.

"Hi Lucy," he said with his slow smile. My hormones must be acting up because he kept getting cuter and cuter each time I saw him. "I brought something over, you know, sorta of a Welcome-to-California basket." He held up a large basket filled with California dates, figs, oranges, almonds, biscuits, music CDs with Californian themes.

"This is wonderful!" I said.

"See," a small voice behind Josh said. "I knew she would love it."

"Hi Jenny," I said, "I love it! That was a cute idea. Something for everyone. Hey you two, come on into my humble abode," I announced. I forgot I was still carrying Grandma's pastry puffs in my right hand. "Oh, have one of these. They're fresh. Grandma and Peter just made them."

They both came in.

"These are great!" Josh said, after taking a bite out of one of them."

"That's good to hear because that's what Grandma loves doing - cooking up yummy things! She and Grandpa ran one of the most popular Chinese restaurants in New York's Chinatown. That was before she came to live with us after my father disappeared." I stopped. I shouldn't have let them known about that! I quickly changed the subject. "Here's our workroom, well, Mom's studio," I said, indicating Mom's mini-studio.

"Wow!" Josh said, looking at Mom's paintings in the room. "These are wonderful!" Then he stopped. "Lucy Lee," he said. "Is your mother Jacqueline Lee?"

"Yes, the one and only," Mom said, walking into the studio with Renee and Elsie in tow. "I couldn't help overhearing."

"Pleasure to meet you," Josh said to my Mom. "I'm Josh Cromwell, and this is my sister Jenny. I have one of your paintings at home."

"Now I like this one already," Mom said to me. "Please to meet a fellow art enthusiast and someone who actually bought one of my paintings," Mom laughed.

"Good," I said. "Now that everyone is acquainted. Oh, Renee and Elsie, you know Josh and Jenny, don't you?" Renee and Elsie nodded. "And vice versa, Josh and Jenny, you know Renee and Elsie?" They shook their heads. "Well, there'll be plenty of time after we get through the meeting to socialize and eat so no worries." I took a breath as everyone took a seat.

"The reason why we're having this meeting right now is not just for the Fall Festival," I said, "but it's also a meeting for us to be called for action. We all know about the tragedy this morning, and I can say for myself, I've been personally moved and touched. I'm sure you have been, too, to some extent. We had a prayer meeting this morning at Crossroads Church, and that made me realize we all have to band together, work together, and lift each other." I took a breath. "That's why I propose that we begin constructing a quilt made up of our expressions, kids' expressions, about America, about what America means to us, about the tragedy, and about hope. We can create a quilt from our school and invite schools from each state in the U.S. to create a quilt of their own. When we have all the quilts, we can piece all the quilts together into a larger quilt. This will be called, 'The Liberty Quilt,' and it will be displayed proudly first in New York and then in Washington D.C."

"That's a great idea!" Mom said.

"We can get the students in the 6th grade to start working on it," Elsie said. "We'll put out a box where any student can contribute a drawing, words, or poem about the tragedy, and create quilt pieces from each."

"We can reveal the school's quilt at the Fall Festival," Renee said.

"Exactly," I said smiling. "How about this theme for the Fall Festival? - American Revolution - Liberty and Justice For All?"

"Yes," Jenny piped up. "That would be fun! We can all dress in colonial outfits. People can play the role of the Founding Fathers…we can have apple cider, pecan pie, all sorts of treats - like the old colonial days."

Josh said, "I'll help get the word out about the Liberty Quilt, and the call for schools across the nation to participate." He smiled. "I think Dad's influence in the entertainment world can accomplish that."

Jenny laughed. "Finally, something worthy to put on the news at Dad's network."

"So," I said. "Everyone likes this idea?"

A resounding 'Yes!' came from everyone.

Inwardly, I gave a sigh of relief. I had no idea my idea was going to go over so well with everyone.

Grandma suddenly appeared at the door to the studio. "Lu-cee, phone for you," she said.

I excused myself and ran to the phone. "Hi," I said.

"Lucy?" a small voice asked. "This is Josie."

"Josie!" I practically shouted into the handset, loud enough to wake the dead. "How is everything?"

"Lucy," Josie said. "They found Father in the rubble."

I held my breath. Dear God, please help Mr. Beretti be alive.

"He's in the hospital. He's badly hurt. Some debris fell on him, but he's still breathing." Josie stopped. "God must have been watching out for him today because he came inches to having his head crushed." Josie lost her resolved, and started crying. "I don't know what we would do if Father had moved his head a few inches to his right. Mother's pretty upset right now."

"Josie," I said. "I know. It's such a scary thought, but that's what it is," I said. "A thought. At least your father's still alive."

"I know," Josie said, wiping her nose with a tissue. "Sorry," she said, "I didn't mean to blow my nose over the phone."

"It's gross, but that's okay," I said. "Just appreciate and cherish each moment you have with your family. I think that's what I've learned today. It's just too bad that it took such a tragedy for us to realize this."

"I know," Josie said. "I mean, now I know somehow what you went through with your father. Only you don't know if he's still alive and if so, where."

"I could barely remember how he looked," I said. "It happened so long ago. So take care of your father, Josie. At least you have one," I said.

"I'm sorry," Josie said again. "I didn't mean to bring up anything that would hurt you. But now, you know what's going on with me and my folks. Take care," Josie said. "When this is all over, we'll talk about happier things, okay?"

"Okay," I said. "Bye." I held the phone for a while longer before placing it back down on the cradle. Josie's call brought up old memories of my father, as well as lots of unresolved questions. Was my father still alive? If so, where?

I didn't realized that I was away from the meeting for a while until Elsie and Renee came over to my side. "Great start!" Renee said. "I'm sure you're going to do alright at school." She giggled. "You even got Jenny to like you. Reputation around school has it that she's the most stuck up girl in town, but now we've seen a part of her that isn't so bad. You should have heard her in there after you left the room. She couldn't stop praising you, and she couldn't stop eating all that wonderful pastry puffs and Chinese snacks your grandmother brought in, after you left the room."

"Not to mention Josh." Elsie said smiling. "My prediction," she closed her eyes and then opened them. "He's probably going to ask you out on a *date* date very soon."

"Nah," I blushed. "We're just friends. Besides, I'm still too young to date."

Elsie and Renee giggled. "Well, we hate to leave, but we should. Both of our parents would have the police out if we're not home in time for dinner," Renee said. "See you at school tomorrow!"

"See you tomorrow," I said, as I saw them to the door. When I returned to the studio, Josh was in deep conversation with Mom. Maybe the girls were mistaken. Josh may be interested in another Lee, as in my mother.

Josh glanced up at me with his smile, clearly enjoying himself, and looked back at my mother. Nah, he wouldn't smile at me like that if he was interested in Mom. Gosh, I wished my hormones would stop making me into a basket case. Next, I'll be thinking he's interested in Grandma!

Jenny approached me. "Lucy, I really like your idea about the Liberty Quilt," she said. "That's a really bold idea, and I don't think I would've gone through with it."

"What do you mean?" I asked.

"I mean," Jenny began. "I couldn't pull off something like that. You could. You're bold, confident, pretty, creative, and nice - everything I'm not! That's why I didn't like you at first. But as I got to know you, and heard what Josh said of you, I began to like you. I guess I was a little jealous."

"Oh," I was surprised. Josh said nice things about me? What??? I almost screamed. "Jenny, I'm no one to be jealous of," I said emphatically. "You should have seen me yesterday before school - I was a nervous wreck!"

"You were?" Jenny asked. Then she said lamely. "I'm really sorry about the way I behaved towards you yesterday at the bus stop and at school. I hope we can be friends."

I smiled. "I'd like that." I smiled even wider. "I'd like that very much." In a matter of two days, God had already answered my prayers.

As Jenny and Josh finally left for home, I climbed back up the stairs and into my room. I went to my dresser drawer, clasped my golden heart necklace around my neck, and headed for my bag of outfits. When I found the safari jacket and shorts, I pulled them out. I smiled a secret smile. Didn't Mom say that Dad disappeared into the jungle on an expedition in Africa? Well, I knew where my next adventure would take me.

Epilogue

The attack on September 11, 2001 was one of the largest attacks the United States of America had ever experienced on American soil. It was estimated that close to 5000 lives were lost in the World Trade Center area alone and that over 200 lives were lost in the Pentagon. No one knows for sure the total exact number of casualties, but the impact affected all American across the entire United States of America.

What You Can Do

To help in the recovery efforts or to aid future relief efforts, you can help by donating blood, food, blankets, toys, or money to a reputable organization such as The American Red Cross or the United Way of NYC.
American Red Cross
1-800-HELP-NOW

United Way of New York City
2 Park Avenue
New York, NY 10016

If you need to talk to someone about the events of September 11, you can talk to an adult you trust such as a teacher, your pastor, your parents, and/or counselors from the American Red Cross at 1-866-GET-INFO.

Please note: Sparklesoup Studios is not affiliated with the American Red Cross or the United Way. By voluntary choice, the publishers of *Lucy and The Liberty Quilt* will donate a portion of the net proceeds of this book to The American Red Cross.

Excerpt from Book 2
of the Gifted Girls Series:

Lucy and The Beauty Queen

The room grew dark, and I found myself no longer in my sunshine yellow bedroom in Southern California, but outside in the middle of a desert. A red sun about to set, stared straight at me. The path went up and down, up and down.

"Go," a dark man dressed in a long brown cotton robe said next to me. He slapped the animal I was riding on to move faster. I glanced down. A large tan furry head with large eyes glanced back at me. I was riding on top of a camel!

I looked around me. There were other people riding on top of camels beside me. An older man with wild white hair and a white beard, a young woman with long wavy auburn hair, a thin-faced man with a patch over his right eye, a brawny young man with blond hair, and a finely-dressed young man with wavy brown hair. Except for the brown-haired young man, everyone was dressed from head to toe as I was: khaki shorts and jackets with hiking boots and safari hats. Dark men dressed in long brown robes walked besides each camel, urging them forward. Some camels carried boxes of supplies.

"Excuse me," I whispered to the young woman with wavy auburn hair, "do you know where we're going?"

The young woman laughed, "if my calculations are correct, we should be heading straight to the Hidden Tomb of Egypt's most famous Queen... Cleopatra."

"Cleopatra?" I asked. "As in the Queen of the Nile?"

"Yes," the beautiful young woman said with an unmistakable British accent. "I see you've actually cracked open your history book for once, my young Cousin Lucy," she joked.

"Muriel!" the old man with the wild white hair shouted. "The men are getting hungry, and it's getting late. We have to make a stop soon."

"Alright, Father," Muriel shouted back. "I could go on and on, can't you?" She took a deep breath. "I love this Egyptian open air. Quite a change from the stuffy, drafty London air we have back home."

The well-dress young man wearing a sportscoat and riding pants rode his camel up to Muriel and I. "Muriel," he said politely. "I wouldn't want anything to happen to you all alone out here with all these men and nasty animals. I'd like to suggest that you pitch your tent next to mine."

Muriel's back straightened. "I'm perfectly capable of taking care of myself, thank you, Roger," she said firmly, "And I'm not 'here all alone'." She smiled. "Have you forgotten, I have my cousin Lucy!"

I looked over at Roger and smiled my widest, smuggest smile. Roger's lips curled, and he left without a word of good-bye. Muriel and I looked at each other and burst into laughter.

The group of travelers and camel handlers soon came to a stop at the foot of a cliff with some palm trees.

As we got off our camels, and the men began setting up camp, I wandered near the palm trees, searching for water. A few feet away from the trees, I found a swimming hole with fruit trees and birds. As I reached up to grab one of the ripe black figs from one of the trees, I heard Muriel's voice shout, "Watch out, Lucy!"

I looked up to see Muriel's anxious face looking at

the fig I was holding, only this time I realized it was not
a fig but a large fuzzy poisonous tarantula spider as big as
my hand!

The Gifted Girls Series™

**Don't miss any of the Gifted Girls' Adventures!
Order or Reserve Your Very Own Copy Today by Mail
or online at http://<u>www.sparklesoup.com</u>**

$7.95 each.
___ **Lucy and the Liberty Quilt: Book 1**
___ **Lucy and the Beauty Queen: Book 2**
   (*Coming in January!*)
___ **Emily Cobbs and The Naked Painting: Book 1**
Join Emily Cobbs, a Gifted Girl from turn-of-the-century
(20th Century) England, who has a gift with the brush.
(*Coming in February!*)

**Sparklesoup Studios
P.O. Box 2285, Frisco, TX 75034**

Please send me the books I have checked above. I am
enclosing
$_____ (please add $2.50 to cover shipping and
handling). Send check or money order - no cash or
C.O.D.'s please.

Name_____

Address_____

City_____State/Zip_____

Email Address_____
Please allow four to six weeks for delivery.

Join the Gifted Girls Club!

Log onto http://www.sparklesoup.com and sign up!

Find out interesting trivia about each Gifted Girl, learn about the people, places and times in history a Gifted Girl visits. Be the first to receive the latest Gifted Girl books, jewelry, stationary, dolls, and fun fashion accessories!